SAYING GOODBYE

J DARK

Cover design copyright © 2019 by Niki Lenhart
nikilen-designs.com

Published by Paper Angel Press
paperangelpress.com

ISBN 978-1-957146-51-5 (Trade Paperback)

10 9 8 7 6 5 4 3 2 1

FIRST EDITION

This story is another deeply personal one that came about after a friend passed suddenly away. It percolated for a while, then burst forth. This one went ninety percent complete about two days after I started it. It consumed me up to the point where the main character drives out to Big Bend Park. Despite only taking a few days to nearly complete, this is one I had to walk away from often, to calm down and let the story out. It was a series of manic spurts and periods of time away to let the emotions settle enough to start writing again. It was a catharsis for me; I purged a lot of grief and anger in the words.

PART ONE

Lightning Crashes
Live

D O YOU KNOW HOW you're going to say goodbye to someone? Is it going to be a loving embrace and a soft caress of their cheek before they go to the great beyond? Or, is it going to be heated words and a pistol stuck in their belly as they try to argue, or to plead with you, not to pull the trigger? Or is it simply a call in the night? A quick stop at the mortuary to look at a lump of flesh bloated with formaldehyde, because that's the law? Or, will you, like me, wonder what happened when they just disappear? Here one day, and gone the next, and no clue where.

I remember — or think I do — the last time I saw Mom and Dad. They'd dropped me off at Uncle Soap's apartment after packing the beat-up gold Ford Taurus for a camping trip. They often went camping alone at least twice a month — down in the Big Bend National Park. I remember Dad wearing his red-and-black-checked shirt he'd pulled the sleeves off. Mom always told him that was her favorite shirt of his. She'd wear it around the house sometimes to tease Dad. Not that they were all sweetness and love. More than once I heard them screaming back and forth about all sorts of things. Almost always it was about drugs.

I didn't understand then, but I think I do now.

They argued the most just before they went camping, and were best together after they got back. As a child, I saw the change, and knew it had something to do with them going camping, but it really didn't matter. Mom and Dad were happy. They paid attention to me, and bought me things like a new set of shoes, or a cool shirt. It's funny that I remember the clothes, but not their faces. I remember Dad always being skinny, and he had fuzz on his face. I don't remember if it was a beard or mustache, both, or if he just didn't shave every day. Mom was like Dad — skinny.

When they didn't go camping, Dad stayed home nights with me while Mom went to work. She'd always dress up in baggy pants and a shirt, and carry lots of bright, flashy clothes that fit in a little carry bag to work. Dad would stay awake with me until I got tired, then I'd get tucked into bed on the couch at the far end of the trailer. I'd fall asleep listening to Dad watch television.

Every so often, before I passed out, I'd watch him give himself a shot of 'medicine' in between his toes. I know he was shooting up now, but then I knew he was always more happy afterwards, so it seemed a good thing to me. I knew something was off — most four-year-olds can sense things. We're not yet aware enough of how to lie to ourselves and avoid uncomfortable truths. Denial and delusion aren't something that's learned right away.

Mom dressed all the time in old clothes and dark colors. When we went out to the store, it was usually in the very early morning. Mom always told me that it was best, because there weren't many people around, and it made shopping easier. Looking back, I think it was because at those hours, hardly anyone she had met at her 'job' would be around. She table-danced, or stripped — whichever describes it best for you.

Mom hated it, and came home crying a lot. That would make Dad unhappy and those were when the biggest fights happened. About her job. About the money she brought home because dad couldn't work. About him not working. They always fought about that. They didn't pay much attention to me then. I learned to hide in my room when their voices started to get an edge. It meant that things were going to get broken, and a lot of slapping and throwing. It was better in my bedroom.

As I look at the memory of it, that room was my refuge — the one place I had some little privacy of my own. It wasn't sacrosanct. Both mom and dad would come in to wake me up, or yell at some accident, or even hide from one another, either in play or … you know. The not-fun-not-play stuff like fighting or yelling or crying. Dad did it a little more than mom. He'd charge in and slam the door, then lean against it. Mom would pound a few times, then go quiet. Dad watched me as he leaned on the door. He'd hold his first finger to his lips and go *"shhhh"*.

I took the hint and leaned silently against the door with him. I barely came to his waist as I pushed to hold the door closed. Dad grinned lopsidedly at me. Mom would pound on the door until she got tired, then go into their room and lock the door. Then dad would open my door, and go back to watching TV, or make some crummy sandwich from whatever was in the fridge.

Other times, it was mom who ran into the room. She'd lock the door like dad, then push my bed against the door. My bed being the futon mom and dad got for me to lay on. One side smelled like smoke and vomit, making me want to throw up too. If I turned it over, then it smelled moldy. I snuck a blanket into my room and put that on top of the moldy side. I wasn't moldy then, just damp and moldy smelling.

Mom, toward that last day I saw them, began taking medicine earlier and more often. She needed it, she said, because the management said that the dancers ("entertainers", mom said) had to show customers a real good time if they got asked. Mom said she didn't like it because it made her feel icky all over, and the medicine made the icky not bother her so much.

In crude adult language, mom was supposed to go have sex with men who paid the manager for the privilege. That's what I found out later. I knew mom felt bad whenever she had to be 'friendly'. She'd come home, throw her purse and dancer's bag on the floor, then run into the bathroom and throw up in the toilet.

Dad would get upset that mom was sick. He'd yell that she should stop working that 'shirthole' of a place. Mom said he couldn't get a job, so she had to work there. They would start arguing about everything. I would go to bed, falling asleep to the shouts. I would wake up in the morning and hold my tummy because I knew they were unhappy. It was like the moldy spot on the futon: mom and dad felt moldy. Dad started taking medicine a lot more too. He would drink until he giggled, then get the needle medicine and stick it in his toe. He bit down on a sock or a pencil because that hurt more.

It was then that the scary man came to the house. Mom and dad looked scared when he showed up. They sent me into my room. He watched me walk all the way to the door. I knew this because I watched him; I looked back over my shoulder all the way. He scared me so much that I didn't want to turn my back to him. His eyes reminded me of the monsters dad giggled at when he was drinking. The red eyes scared me more than anything. I kept waking up thinking he was in the room with me. Mom and dad didn't like that, and I had to stand outside on the front stoop until they let me back in after the sun came up.

But, despite all the troubles, I felt loved. My parents paid attention to me. Not always kind and friendly — they sometimes punished me for things I didn't understand — but they gave me attention all the time. At the age I was, attention was always welcome, even if pain was part of it. Mom and Dad were gods. They fed me, housed me, and, on occasion, actually loved me. It was a place I knew I belonged. The troubles went away after the scary man came.

Mom and Dad started going out camping together. Both came back happy. Both gave me attention that made me happy. It was exciting. Neither of them were fighting any more. The bad old days had disappeared with the visit by the scary man. I got things. Toys. Clothes. Not just new clothes, but new clothes so stiff they itched me. They had funny tags on them. The food was sweeter, and there was more of everything.

PART TWO

Far Behind
Candlebox

MOM AND DAD WOULD GO OUT CAMPING a lot over the next year, according to Uncle Soap. He would take care of me while they were away on the weekends. Uncle Soap was a short, round man with white wisps of hair making him look like the character from the Back to the Future cartoons, only not quite as tall or skinny. He was always talking to himself. All day long he would mutter about rain, about warming, about trash overload, and people overload. I think he was a researcher of some kind.

His apartment was more cluttered than mom and dad's — only it was paper. Paper was everywhere. Newspapers stacked nearest the door. Sometimes they would be a whole stack; other days almost nothing. In the small living room, there were so many stacks of paper that it was a maze. Uncle Soap had paths to the TV, to the kitchen, to his old yellow sofa he slept on, to the bathroom, to the faded blue easy chair with a brown stain where I threw up when I was sick once, and to a locked door at the very back of the house that he never opened while I was there with him.

Uncle Soap was a good man. I liked going to see him. He was never cross or angry at me, and he never hit me about anything.

He answered any questions I had about anything. He always watched out for me. The attention was so much that it was like he was smothering me on some days. I'd go hide in the small square of empty space just behind the faded blue easy chair, and look at the newspapers, imagining tall white buildings that things went on in: a person making a stamp, and stamping out comics.

The back window was actually a sliding glass door. It had stacks of paper all the way across the bottom that were as tall as my chin when I looked out. The old brown curtains reminded me of mom and dad's linoleum floor back home. I could part the curtains and look out into a cement back yard with a strip of ground that was an amazing green color. All the grass in that strip was the same height, and a lush texture that didn't look at all like the ground around mom and dad's trailer.

The ground around the trailer was brown, mostly. Small single plants poked up out of the dirt here and there, looking like grasping hands to me. I didn't like the yard, and stayed inside when I could. Mom and dad would make me go outside when they wanted quiet time. Everything around the trailer, and the other broken-down trailers, made me think of animals crawling off to die.

Which is what trailer parks remind me of whenever I drive by one. They're not dead-ends for broken dreams; there are many families that do well. It's my own memories that create the image that I see whenever I pass by one. The trailer park we lived in, the *Western Spur*, was truly the last refuge of broken dreams and wasted lives.

I didn't like it, but children can adapt, and I was able to make some friends, or make up others when the few other kids like me weren't around. Being the youngest meant that I was always the last one to be able to do anything if I was in a group. That was, I think, what made me value time alone. I didn't have to wait, and I didn't have to do what the bigger kids wanted to. I could go at my own pace, explore what interested me, and not what someone else decided was the thing to go do.

It was kind of how mom and dad were after the scary man came by. They quit seeing friends, except for Uncle Soap, and kept the curtains pulled so there wasn't any way to look outside.

They still put me out to play, but it wasn't the same. Most of the other kids had moved away, or were now in school, so there was no one to play with, and I wasn't enrolled in kindergarten. So that meant I spent most of my home time alone outdoors.

My days were being pushed outside when my parents woke up, being given money to go to the little general store at the entrance of the park, buy a snack for lunch, and then stay outside until the afternoon, when mom and dad let me back in to play in the house, eat dinner, watch TV, and then go to sleep, to do it all over again the next day.

This went on, until the day that next spring. Mom and dad dropped me off at Uncle Soap's. I don't know if it's me looking back and trying to put some prescient thought into that day in my mind, or I did actually pick up that my parents were more excited than usual for a camping weekend.

I remember them dropping me off the usual way, by honking the horn on the old gold Ford Taurus, and waiting for Uncle Soap to walk out. Once he waved at them, mom shifted the car in drive, dad yelled, "G'bye kid! See you Sunday!", and turned up the radio. With music blaring from the car, mom drove out of the parking lot, turned right, and disappeared behind the red brick wall at the entrance to the apartment complex. That was the last time I saw them.

When they did not show up Sunday night, Uncle Soap became worried. He paced more than usual. He talked to himself and walked over to the pink-colored telephone on the stack of papers nearest the kitchen entrance. He picked the receiver up, then tapped away at it. He growled into the mouthpiece, then listened intently. His face flushed red and he looked more like a mad scientist as he picked up the body of the phone, pacing in agitation back and forth in the little kitchen. He screamed at the other person, then slammed the handle back down on the body, and, with exaggerated care, placed it back on the stack of papers.

That was the first night without my parents. I stayed awake all night waiting to hear the familiar mutter of the car's engine, and mom beeping the horn. It never happened. I wasn't worried. I did recognize the change in routine, but being with Uncle Soap made the unusual situation bearable. Uncle Soap was really good at putting me at ease. That sense of comfort dissolved with the next angry phone call to whomever he was talking to. His yelling was louder than mom and dad, so I hid in the stacks of papers until he stopped yelling.

The days began to set a rhythm: early morning breakfast of cereal and bacon, lunch of a processed meat and cheese, and dinner consisting of hamburgers from the local fast-food shop nearby.

Uncle Soap spent most of his time hunched over the personal computer he had set on the round table in the middle of some paper stacks in what was a dining room. The chair he sat in creaked and squeaked constantly. He fidgeted all the time. I didn't really notice it until after my parents never came back. Then, everything was magnified. I wanted to go home, and see my mom and dad, and this desire made everything harder to cope with. By the end of the week, I had taken to hiding in the stacks of paper, and not coming out except to eat.

I think it might have gone on that way, but a short while after Uncle Soap and I started having troubles, Social Services stepped in.

PART THREE

Saturday Night's All Right for Fighting
Elton John

M Y FAMILY HAD BEEN GONE ABOUT TWO WEEKS, and no one had seen them. Uncle Soap's calls to the police had raised flags, which brought Social Services in. They immediately declared Uncle Soap's place "unlivable".

Despite loud and angry protests from both me and Uncle Soap, I was taken away by a woman in a blue dress suit and a man in a brown suit. I can still see them. It was one of the most traumatic days of my life. I was hauled off, under the man's arm, and placed in the back of a white car. The doors locked immediately when the man closed the door.

The details are stark, and fuzzy, at the same time. The terror of being torn away from the only family I'd known was almost overwhelming. I could only think about escaping. When the man in the brown suit finished driving to the orphanage, I darted as quickly as I could towards the open door. I was caught easily by the man, who had been expecting this. I was corralled as easily as one might think a five-year-old would be when trapped in the back seat of an automobile.

The man grabbed me by the hair and around my waist. His grip on my hair kept me from biting him, which he'd probably had experience with before. He yanked on my hair as I struggled, keeping my neck and back arched as he carried me to a small room. It was a pale blue, and had a table, two chairs, an overhead light, no windows, and only one door.

He stepped into the open doorway, dropping me in the room, and remaining while I glared at him. He told me to sit in the far chair and wait until my "case worker" could talk to me. I remember him saying, "Bye, kid." Then he closed the door. I never saw him again.

The case worker startled me by knocking on the door. Her voice was quiet, and reminded me of a mouse. She asked if she could come in to talk to me, ignoring my loud "No!" by opening the door and stepping through. She closed the door behind her, locking it. I knew attempting escape would be fruitless; I couldn't get through the door.

She sat down in the other seat, tapping the desk with a thin green folder. She had on a business suit that looked like the other woman's blue one, only in pale pink. She had dark brown skin, and an accent that I didn't recognize. She said her name was Bethea, pronounced *Beh-thee-ah*. She talked about how hard it must have been living in that filthy, cluttered apartment. She said that Uncle Soap couldn't take care of me anymore because he wasn't related. I would be sent to a family, a foster home, until they could set me up with a real family who would be willing to adopt me.

I did not want to be adopted and go to a foster home. I wanted to go back to MY home. I wanted to see my mom and dad. I wanted to see Uncle Soap. I wanted to be away from all these strange people.

But my wishes weren't worth anything. The state placed me in a foster home, and it turned into a disaster. It was too soon after losing all the people in my family. I acted out, broke things, attacked the other children, and screamed constantly, until the foster parents threw up their hands and sent me back to the orphanage.

See ya, don't let the door hit you in the ass when you leave.

From there, it was one bad stop after another. Some of it was my fault. I couldn't get past that my parents had left me. I was convinced that they were alive somewhere, enjoying life after ditching me at Uncle Soap's. It was my fault that they left; my fault they never came back. Then it was their fault, and I took my anger out on anyone around me. I told stories, lies, about my parents. That they were secret agents, and had to leave me behind. Or, that they were wealthy beyond imagining, and had to leave me behind to keep me safe from kidnappers.

Each story was more outlandish, more improbable. I told them, because the truth I saw was that they didn't want me. I wanted an excuse that I could have why they didn't want me. The lies were for others, but they were mostly for myself. It hurt, and the hurt settled into a routine of more and more anger and behavior problems leading up to the night that destroyed any chance of me ever being adopted.

I was twelve, and a six-year veteran of the Social Services process. My latest foster family were known as strict, but fair, disciplinarians — supposedly perfect for problem children in the system. I was sent out to them to curb my violent tendencies. The stay lasted one day.

The father, Charley, was a shooting safety instructor, and a former Navy veteran. He was a head taller, and twice as massive, as I was, with black hair sprinkled with grey. His wife and partner, Kris, was my height, and stocky. She had blonde hair, and liked to dress up in fatigues. That was my first infraction: I laughed at her.

Charley immediately grabbed me, slamming me against the wall. He shouted the question, "Did I think it was funny?".

Being rebellious, and not realizing exactly what I had been placed in, I said "Yes."

Charley backhanded me across the face, knocking me into the kitchen.

The kitchen walls were papered in a pale yellow with light, violet-colored flowers. White counter tops ran all the way around from the archway into the kitchen from the living room, making a single gap at the door to the garage, then continuing back around to the archway. A second slap rocked my head to the right, and I saw the butcher's block with all the protruding handles.

I grabbed the chef's knife, and attacked. I think that Charley, for all his self-defense training, expected me to charge in. I did, but pulled up short, and slashed his arm wide open. He screamed, which brought Kris running. She charged into the kitchen, saw Charley's slashed arm, and me with the knife. I remember seeing her eyes harden. Then she reached behind her back like she was going to pull a pistol or knife.

I didn't wait. Two quick steps had me past Charley, and I stabbed Kris low in the stomach. She folded over the knife, and Charley hit me hard from behind.

Say goodbye to the orphanage, and hello to Juvenile Hall.

Kris and Charley hired a lawyer to get me tried as an adult. I later found out I'd killed the baby in her; it was only weeks old. The knife severed the small sac it was growing in. I was sentenced as a juvenile, due to my age, and probably because of the beating Charley gave me after I passed out.

I was sent away to the Palmerton Juvenile Detention Complex.

PART FOUR

What it is
Everlast

I NEVER GOT TO SAY GOODBYE to anyone at the orphanage and, honestly, I didn't much care. The place wasn't home. Palmerton was a lot like home, only bigger — and lots more crowded.

The building was a re-purposed elementary school. There was a map at the entrance, with a "You Are Here" arrow right at midpoint between two large squares. The main entrance was between the two main buildings connected by a long hall that fronted the gymnasium-cafeteria. This made the place look kind of like a dumbbell from overhead. The dorms for the boys were in the west dumbbell; the girls in the east. Never did we see the other side. The powers that be declared us to be unfit for each other's company.

The dorm rooms were crudely bricked in place without altering the original classroom dimensions. A small straight hall ran from the door to the interior rooms, made up in four long rectangles per each former classroom. Two 'guests' shared each room. At capacity, we were told the Palmerton could hold one hundred and twenty of each sex.

Outside was a "rec field". It was two football fields wide, and one long. Sickly green grass grew in patches here and there, seemingly at random. There were no trees. The back wall was fifteen feet of smooth cement with coiled razor wire at the top. Cameras were mounted on each of the corner towers, which also controlled eight drones that hovered and darted overhead.

I still had vague memories of mom and dad, yelling, and a place with a lot of dry dirt around what we lived in. Palmerton was a lot like that, and I fit in there more than anywhere else since I had been taken away from Uncle Soap.

Everyone was out for themselves, and that suited me just fine. It was fight, or get bullied; predator, or prey. I wasn't an alpha, but I was close. No one fought with me if they didn't have to, and the perks for protecting others from some of the lower-level predators kept me in things like flasks of alcohol, cigarettes, iPods ... you get the picture.

I was the guest of Palmerton until I turned eighteen, and then my juvenile records were sealed, and I was kicked out onto the streets, with an obligatory stay in a "halfway house" to help me re-integrate with the world.

Truth be told, I was reluctant to leave Palmerton. I'd had a sweet setup there, and saying goodbye was like being taken away from Uncle Soap all over again.

The halfway house was a surprise — I mean a real surprise. The halfway house, called The Draper Center, was a series of four triplex homes nested at the end of a *cul-de-sac*. Whoever sent me there also sent my juvenile records. I don't know if that's standard or not. All I know is the boss, one Kesha Harkasse — whom everyone referred to as "Hardcase", took me aside, in an eerie replay of my confrontation with Charley.

She slammed me against the wood-paneled walls, compressing my chest with a finger the size of a bratwurst sausage, and snarled whether I was going start trouble by trying to stab her staff?

Her glare, and the taser in her other hand, convinced me not to smart-mouth.

She got a quiet, "No."

Thereafter, every day we checked in for work around the house. Things like cleaning toilets, mowing the yard, cleaning up gardens, painting, basic carpentry, and actually learning plumbing, filled my day from morning to mid-afternoon. Then, we gathered for lunch, talked about our past. Needless to say, no one really opened up about much.

Hardcase kept a sharp eye on me, and on a lot of the other kids. I didn't like her much after our first little chat, but she did keep everyone on their toes: working, studying, and getting ready to head out of the Draper and into the big, wide, scary, real world.

It was a month after I started there, that Harold "Hal" Matchick "graduated". Hardcase called us all together in the main house of the Draper, and announced that Hal's mandatory stay was completed. He'd found a mechanic's job away from any former relationships, and away from any other ex-cons. He had full-time employment, and would be heading back to school on a scholarship of some kind. He'd really tried hard and it paid off, big-time.

Hardcase got a cake, and soda (no booze, because that's against policy), and snacks. It actually was a good time, and the good-bye party really was like he had gotten over the hump and on his way back to a real life away from Juvie — and especially away from the real prison system. For one shining moment, we saw a dream come true.

That night, with the glow of the dream still alive in me, I saw a chance to change. Hal had made it; that meant I could make it. I just had to buckle down a little and get with the program. Some of the guys were already talking about doing the same thing I was thinking about: getting serious about the future. It's said that nothing breeds success like success, and we'd seen it first-hand, and wanted our own success story.

There's another old saw that says, "No good deed ever goes unpunished." That's what happened that night, but we didn't learn about it until weeks later. Hardcase thought the information would be too devastating so soon after seeing Hal pull it off. She kept it to herself, and the staff kept it in the dark too.

The story is Hal had gone home that night, to see his folks, and share the good news. He took a taxi to his folks, on the edge of Groveland. Groveland was a viciously poor part of town, made up of winding roads, old dying trees, and old base housing for the former wiring factory.

Hal got out of the taxi and was immediately spotted by old acquaintances in the 'hood. These belonged to a different gang than Hal did when he went into Juvie. Hal had 'tuned up' a couple of them before going in. Grudges die hard on the streets. This one was no exception. They got together and stole a car, then parked across the street from Hal's folks. As the taxi pulled up, Hal waved goodbye to his folks. That was the last thing he did.

The crew in the car opened up with pistols and a semi-auto-shotgun. The 'double-oh' buckshot knocked him down. Hal was hit by a number of rounds, both buckshot and nine-millimeter. He was dead before he finished falling. His parents were killed in the barrage, and his sister had her legs paralyzed by a stray nine-millimeter round that passed through the siding and lodged in her spine. It was one of those "What the heck?" things that you expect in a book, but not in real life.

PART FIVE

Drift Away
Uncle Kracker/Dobie Gray

NOT KNOWING OF HAL'S MURDER at the time, I'd taken his example to heart. I pushed a little harder, worked on my GED classes, just like Hardcase wanted. I started going out more, looking at jobs. I talked to people rather than fought with them. It was different, weird. My whole world changed from one made with insults and fists.

I wasn't always looking over my shoulder for enemies. Now it was people genuinely pleased to see me — Hardcase most of all. With my metamorphosis, she changed too. One change fed the other, I guess.

The fact is that we — and I mean most of us in the Draper — actually looked forward to getting a new chance. Hal's example gave that to us. Hardcase was smart enough to keep the ball rolling and, instead of one, she had seven of us ex-juvenile delinquents that had seemingly changed our ways. I say "seemingly" because, after I "graduated" from the Draper, I lost track of everyone.

That's deliberate, by the way. No ties means no temptation; no one pulling you back into the life you had before. A clean break in every way. For me, it worked. I got my GED while at the Draper, and the party was for three of us. There was a lot of swapping stories and back-slapping kind of stuff. This was a goodbye to remember. Hardcase had to still get on us about our work, and she promised "holy hell" in spades if we backslid. I miss her.

I think her "tough-but-fair" attitude replaced my idea of what a mom was. Even now, I look at her as the mom I hadn't had before. It's a warm, nostalgic feeling, filled with little things like coffee in the morning, cleaning dishes — stuff you overlook in the normal course of a day. They mean more now, a good warm memory that overrides the harsh comparison with my own folks.

Because my records were sealed at eighteen, I had no criminal record as an adult. I gravitated to firefighting, convinced that was the best fit for me. Six months and four days later, I graduated third in my class. I got assigned to Firehouse Fifty-Eight, ironically, out near my folks' old trailer park. I didn't think much of it at first. Fire calls kept me busy, and the daily routine of cleaning the trucks, checking equipment, and going to the gym to push my strength, occupied my days fully.

It was the week-on, week-off routine that started me on my personal quest to find out what happened that night. At loose ends again while off-duty had me search for a way to fill the time. I got into camping. Big Bend isn't all that far away: just head east on Interstate Ten, then turn on State Ninety and, an hour later, you're at the entrance. There are always plenty of places to camp and hike. I got a metal detector too.

I'd read about all those people finding old coins in the ground, and thought that would be a way to spend the time during camping. Find a spot to camp, then wander about with the metal detector and see what I'd find. I got lucky right off, finding an Eisenhower dollar under about a foot of sand in a dry wash. Then it became more of small discoveries, like a jar lid, a rusted can, tossed pull tabs, thrown beer cans, and some loose change. All of this, I think, was me attempting in some way to connect with my parents.

I'd lay in my sleeping bag out under the stars in the bed of my pickup and wonder at the sky. Did my folks look at it the same way I did? Were they still around? I didn't think they were, but hope springs eternal.

It was six months after I'd started my camping habit, that the bug got me. Someone, somewhere, had to know something. The most obvious choice would be those who hung around my folks, and the most obvious one was Uncle Soap.

Ten years is a long time to lose contact, but Uncle Soap was surprisingly easy to find. He still lived in the same apartment, with all the same cluttered stacks of papers and barely wide-enough trails between them to the front door and the other places in the cramped one-bedroom. That I remembered his real name was a surprise. I never remembered hearing it. But Sonomorous Apijillo was unique enough to stay buried in my memories until the search began.

Despite his name, Uncle Soap didn't know a word of Spanish. I've never heard him utter one word of it. During my search for him, I found out a few things that made sense, given what I remembered of Uncle Soap. He was a researcher, primarily focused on political trends. He never worked anywhere except on the internet. He used a number of privacy sites to keep his ID hidden away from detractors and disgruntled employers.

In short, Uncle Soap loved to throw his opinion (usually well thought out and documented) at his employers — whether they wanted the truth or not. He was one researcher that didn't slant his work, and this "quirk" had gotten him a lot of research gigs for large companies — and a lot of irritation from the same companies because of his refusal to write "favorable" reports about their activities and attempts at influencing the public. He was, in his own quirky way, a bit like Diogenes: shining a lamp and looking in the corners of the 'net for the truth.

The day I went to see Uncle Soap started warm, and heated up from there. It was past the one-hundred mark on the thermometer when I pulled into the old apartment complex. The stucco walls were cracked. Here and there some paint had been slap-dashed on over caulking, but the difference between the fresh coat and the old faded one made the place look like a patchwork of shades of brown. The sidewalk slanted to the right as I started into the complex from the dirt parking lot. Dust kicked up with my steps until I reached the angled concrete.

It was so familiar that I shivered, regressing to the lonely, angry nine-year-old that I'd been. The screams of rage, and the feel of the social worker's hold on me was real around my waist. My breath shortened as my heart sped up. It took some deep breaths to slow my mind down and to banish the ghosts that choked my breath.

It was with a lot of mixed feelings that I walked to Number Fourteen and knocked. Uncle Soap opened the door to the extent of the safety chain, and then peered out at me. His face was much like I remembered: rounded, with grey three-day-old stubble, a balding head, and a rotund body that was more gaunt than my memories of him. He blinked bloodshot eyes, and grumbled if I had the right address.

When I didn't answer right away, he glared at me, and asked if I was a dumbass mute. In truth, I couldn't answer. I'd started choking up the moment the door had opened. The tears running down the edge of my nose caught his attention. His irritation gave way to puzzlement, then a dawning realization. His eyes widened. The door slammed shut in my face, the chain was noisily unlatched, then the door all but flew open as Uncle Soap stared hard at my face, his own eyes going misty with recollection.

Tears began leaking along his nose as he reached for me, fingers brushing my cheek. He was so small. In the intervening years, I'd grown, and now overtopped him by a full head and shoulders — a far cry from looking up at the big, round man of my youth. The fierce hug broke the dam, and I folded over his shoulder, crying my heart out as his own tears soaked the front of my t-shirt. I was a child again, and my Uncle Soap was here. Everything was all right.

I don't know how long we embraced, rocking and crying together. It felt like forever, and an eyeblink. Immediate, and timeless. The ghosts of the past wrapped around me like Jacob Marley's chains in *A Christmas Carol*. I couldn't stop now, even if I wanted. The chains of the past weighed too heavily on me to do anything else.

Uncle Soap gave one last, loud sniffle, then pulled me through the faded yellow door, into the world of paper stacks and pathways. Nostalgia rose up like a long-lost friend, and enveloped me in a dry, musty scent, laden with memories.

Still being led by the hand, I followed Uncle Soap through the maze of waist-high stacks of paper to the surprisingly clean and tidy kitchen. It was one of those incongruous things that you might not notice for ages, but Uncle Soap's place, despite the clutter, was actually very neat and clean.

There was no accumulated dust on his stacks of papers, or on the tall Venetian blinds in front of the sliding glass door. Somehow, despite all his clutter, Uncle Soap kept everything free of dust. Seeing this brought a surge of anger towards those long-ago Social Services workers. They took me away from the only family I had. My hands started hurting. I glanced down, seeing blood leaking around my fingers. I'd clenched my hands so hard my fingernails cut my palms.

Uncle Soap noticed too, and his face scrunched up with worry. He asked if I was all right.

That was a real hard question right then. I was tense with suppressed rage at the long-ago hurts, at the social workers, and most at my parents for leaving me behind. It took me a full minute to unclench my hands, and answer Uncle Soap.

He didn't really relax though. His face pulled taut with memories. I could see them flicker with each twitch of his cheek, every shift of his lips. He, like I, was in the grip of those long-ago days that this unexpected reunion had dredged up.

He gripped me tight in a sudden hug, bawling his heart out against my chest. I could feel his anguish in every shuddering catch of his breath. Somewhere in the middle of that, I was crying again, my own harsh sobs mixing with Uncle Soap's, making us sound like wounded animals shrieking for comfort.

I don't know how long we howled our pain into the empty air of the apartment. It was certainly long enough to turn my voice into a ragged, rasping croak. Uncle Soap was no better off. His voice was a sandpapered whisper when he finally tried speaking again.

We sat, heads together, arms about each other like life preservers in storm-tossed seas. We stood silently for a long time, slowly coming to peace with the emotional release that had overwhelmed us. The comfort of another soul that cared was so intense, so encompassing ... it was spiritual. I don't know any other word for it — a spiritual connection, a spiritual healing.

Uncle Soap finally asked me why I came to him. I didn't answer for a long time. It wasn't that I didn't want to; it was because I couldn't. I didn't really know if I wanted to hunt down what happened to my Mom and Dad, for fear of what I might find — or, what I might not.

How would I feel if this was all a dead end? How would I feel if it wasn't? Is knowing better, or worse, than not knowing?

I was so wrapped in memories that I wasn't thinking, being totally immersed in those long-ago emotions of anger, desperation, and loss.

I finally, finally, managed to raise my head to look at Uncle Soap. His red-rimmed eyes were still moist with the remains of shed tears. He asked me again, with a catch in his raw, quiet voice, why I came to see him. It was a decision I'd wrestled enough. For better or worse, I had to know. Now it was my own damaged voice that whispered brokenly about my desire to know. I had to know. That was the only goal in front of me.

We talked: he wanted to test me, to make me certain this path was the one I wanted. I endeavored to convince him it was the only way to let the past go. We both knew it was already determined, but we both needed to make our case, to talk about our reasons — even though we knew they were the same. I guess people just need to talk mindlessly sometimes so that their real thoughts can have a moment to focus.

PART SIX

Tears in Heaven
Eric Clapton

THE SUN WAS SETTING by the time we finished our discussion. Uncle Soap would help where he could, but it was going to be up to me to do the actual hunt. My job would give me access to past reports of incidents in the park, if one had been submitted. His delving into history and open records could uncover reasons, or some kind of activity, that created their disappearance. Knowing that might narrow a search. I thought it a next-to-nothing chance, but the operative word that swayed me was "next". There was a chance.

So we began, and I began to understand why Uncle Soap was so adamant about knowing my reasons. It became an obsession for me almost overnight. My parents. That long-ago creation of the empty hole in me threatened to burst open like an infected bite, and spew it's pain and anger through me once more.

I know I changed. The burning in my mind was something I could not ignore. One of the most powerful things is to have a solid goal, a quest for a holy grail. That was what it became. Every moment was focused towards my desire.

Uncle Soap found a few "trends", as he called them, that made him think that the park was being used for drug drops back in the day. That pulled memories of the scary man, the sudden money, and my parents big mood swings around "camping time". It made sense to me, but Uncle Soap argued that one thing did not make the other true. He needed more information before he'd say anything. I wanted an answer NOW. We fought over every detail he'd dredged up. I was convinced that the drug track was the right track. He wouldn't commit, because it was not definitive, not solid.

It was stupid. I knew it was stupid. My mind wouldn't let go of what I remembered. I refused to believe anything else. More than anything, I wanted my answer. Nothing else was important.

As you might figure, my performance at work suffered, and I relived all the frightening, ugly times that I experienced as a child. I'd turned back into that frightened kid who had been taken away after his parents vanished. All those feelings of loss, betrayal, and hate were with me all the time. My camping trips became crusades to slay the dragons that were consuming me.

I still found things with the metal detector — more coins, cans, and random bits of things. Everything I found hit me with the question: "Was it theirs?" Did my folks lose this camping? Did they camp in this spot, or over at another? What happened out camping?

I found myself seeking out the more remote, wild spots in Big Bend. I was hunting, but still unsure what, in my mind. It might have been to find something that I could definitely call theirs, something to put my faith in that I'd found them after all this time. Up to that point, all I'd found was junk with the metal detector.

Uncle Soap had been doing his "magic" on the internet. He followed up reports turned in by campers in a number of spots in Big Bend, checking for clusters of reports. We knew the weekend they disappeared, and that they were going camping. Incident reports of loud noises or gunshots were sparse due to the lack of wireless communications back then.

There were a few reports that Uncle Soap found in digging through old databases that had been made public. Based on the time they disappeared, he thought there were two places to search. I didn't have any friends, and Uncle Soap wouldn't leave his apartment, so the search fell to me.

A cloudless morning greeted me when I awoke. The still air held the promise of blistering heat as I exited my apartment. The dusty pavement surrounded me in a cloud of brown as I stepped to my pickup and got in. The engine caught immediately, and I backed out of the lot, then turned west towards Big Bend. The knobby tires hummed on the road as the miles disappeared under the wheels and, by mid-afternoon, I was at the Big Bend entrance.

The sun beat down, heat shimmering in front of the truck as I drove towards the first of the two locations. It was a spot I was familiar with. I was focused, ready to tear answers from the ground.

The campsite lay along the slope leading towards the South Rim, nestled at the southeast of the Rim, down near a dry wash. The area had been cleared recently. No scrub grew in or around the campsite. Salt Cedar and a few Willow trees clustered near the dry wash, as if waiting for the next rain. I was out of the cab of my pickup almost before the truck finished moving. The metal detector hung ponderously in my left hand, the headphones in my right. I clapped the phones over my ears and flipped the detector on.

The feedback squeal in my ears felt like spikes into my brain. I gritted my teeth until the detector finished warming up, then hit the discriminator button to select "Relics", and began sweeping. The coil moved back and forth, reminding me of a hound casting for scent. Small beeps teased my ears as I methodically hunted for my past.

After a half hour, I had to stop. I'd been gritting my teeth so hard that my jaw ached. The temperature had gone from a promise, to oppressively hot. Dust hung in the air with no wind to disperse it. It clogged my nose and throat, adding to my misery of the heat. I went back to the truck and pulled a gallon jug of water from behind the passenger seat. Half went to soak my clothes and get rid of the dust; the rest was for me, to keep me hydrated.

Too much water? Not in Big Bend. You do *not* want to get caught with too little water out here. That's how you *die*. All the tension of being so close to my desire had me tramping up through the site and back to isolated corners of it where a car could be buried.

You heard right. Buried. Somewhere I'd become convinced that my parent's car was hidden out here, just under the surface, waiting for me to come along and find it. That's what happens, when you sink your whole self into something without checking your common sense — dreams blow into irrational nightmares that swallow you whole.

I searched all day, over and around the campground. To be thorough, I ran a grid pattern: first north and south fifty paces, with a two-step separation. This made sure I overlapped with the metal detector my previous trace. It wasn't difficult within the campsite area to keep to the north-south lines, but outside the maintained ground, I had more trouble. Brush slowed me and, at times, was impenetrable to walk through. Irregular terrain made things tough, and some places weren't possible to reach.

Sundown splashed orange in the western sky as I reluctantly called a halt to my search. I had a sleeping kit with a large canvas tarp and two posts setting in my pickup bed. The posts went in welded circles at the front of the bed and into a hole at the top of the tailgate just off its center. This made a low tent out of the canvas by simply tying the edges of the tarp to the walls of the pickup. A blow-up sleeping pad in the bed with two wool blankets finished my "tent". I slept in the pickup, rather than on the ground. I don't like snakes, and Big Bend is full of them.

The wind remained still, or nearly so, which was pretty unusual. A typical day in Big Bend had wind, all the time. You were never without it — always trying to push, always shifting. Mild on the open ground, it got fierce in the deep gullies. Not having its constant presence woke me up just after midnight, convinced there was something just outside the tent. No crickets chirped; no coyotes howled — no noise at all. It was like the whole world was holding its breath, waiting.

A vague feeling of dread enveloped me. I sat up in the pickup and poked my head over the top of the tailgate in time to see a car rolling into the campground. It angled left and slewed drunkenly to a stop near my campsite.

The car was a Ford Taurus — an old beat-up nineteen-nineties model, like my parents used to drive. "What it is" by Everlast blared from its open passenger window. The Taurus bobbed and rocked on its tires as the figures inside moved about inside. I tried to stand up to untie the tarp so I could get out, but I was frozen in place. I was not a participant at all, but a silent observer.

The passenger door flung open, then back as it hit the stops and rebounded. A man kicked his foot out to hold the door from closing, like I'd seen so often. Dad.

He looked smaller, and more emaciated, than I remembered. He was wearing his old sleeveless black t-shirt with an orange Jimi Hendrix outline on the front. His faded blue jeans looked so pale to be almost white in the night. Mom slipped gracefully out of the driver's side. She carefully swung the door open, then closed. My breath caught.

She was shorter than I remembered, and thinner. Because of her constant dancing onstage, her body was taut and athletic. She'd discarded the baggy clothes, and was wearing low-rider jeans and Dad's red and black T-shirt. I never really remembered seeing her without all the baggy, shapeless clothing. It was like seeing a butterfly after it had crawled out of a chrysalis. She walked around the front of the car and hugged Dad. They held each other for a long moment before separating.

Dad walked towards the high side of the campground, then nodded, and walked back. He whispered something to Mom, who was pulling the tent out of the trunk. The two of them carried the tent to the area that Dad had looked at earlier, then dropped the tent and commenced setting it up. Once the mushroom-looking tent was assembled, Dad walked back over to the car, pulling a cylinder with three legs on it from the trunk.

He walked halfway back to the tent, yelling something to Mom, who pointed downhill towards the large dry wash. Dad shrugged, and smiled, then trotted down slope. He walked at least of a quarter mile, yet I could see him clearly, as he set the cylinder down on its legs, then pressed a button on the side.

On the top of the cylinder, a red light lit up, and Dad trotted back to the tent, a big grin on his face. He entered the tent where Mom was, and the tent shuddered energetically as they made love to each other. The tent quieted down after a while, and dad trotted back out to the device and turned it off.

He left the device off all the next day as he and Mom stayed around the tent, gathering firewood, built a fire pit from rocks, began drinking, and then shooting up. Through it all I was the silent sentinel, never moving, but always bearing witness.

Dad sat on the biggest rock, his teeth gritted as the needle slid home between the big and middle toes. The plunger depressed as he tilted his head back, a beatific smile forming on his lips as the drug coursed through him. He capped the needle, dropped it in the fire pit, then walked back towards the tent. After he entered it, things sped up. The sun raced across the sky, dropping behind the hills as day shifted to dusk.

A glint in the north sky caught my attention. Then a flash of lightning lit the purple and orange clouds off in the distance to the west. The object in the north reflected the rays of the setting sun as it approached. Mom and Dad's tent spasmed crazily, and Dad came running out, pants half pulled up. He stumble-ran to the object in the dry wash and flipped it on. The red light pulsed faintly as he finished pulling his pants up and ran back towards the tent.

Mom was standing out front, pulling on her black Rolling Stones t-shirt with the huge red lips and tongue on the front, watching the small airplane weave closer now that the signal was active. As the high-wing airplane flew in just above treetop level, a large canvas tarp was pulled back on the passenger side. The plane rolled to its right, and a large square package fell from the plane. A chute attached to the package opened immediately, and the box fell in the dry wash, not fifty yards from the signal device.

Dad and Mom had watched the drop with glee, dancing excitedly in place while the plane flew over. Dad took off for the dry wash as soon as the chute opened, running like mad. Mom followed gingerly; she was barefoot and the ground was uneven, with prickly pear cactus, low spiny brush, and other uncomfortable things that would be painful to step on. She stopped halfway to the dry wash, then turned towards the car, limping over to it, and getting in.

The old Taurus rattled to life, then backed down into the dry wash where Dad was busy untangling the parachute from the box. He pulled a box cutter from his pocket and sawed away at the cords holding the chute and package together. Mom knocked over the cylinder, then hopped out of the car, walking over to turn off the signal device, open the trunk, and place the contraption back inside it. Neither of them paid much attention to their surroundings. The first hint of anything wrong was the trickle of water around their feet.

Dad yelled something at Mom, who splashed to his side. The water was halfway up their calves as they tried to lift the box into the trunk of the Taurus. The water actually helped them reach the bumper, but they didn't have the strength, or the leverage, as the water rose past their knees.

The car rocked as the water began to push it downstream. The motion caught Mom by surprise. The bumper hit her knee. She lost her grip on the package, and disappeared under the water. Dad yelled and dropped the box, which started floating downstream. He turned, reaching for the box with his right arm, while leaning over and searching the water with his left for Mom. The car pushed against him in the waist high current and, for a moment, he held his ground. He abandoned the box and put his desperate effort into finding Mom.

I saw her hand raise up out of the muddy brown torrent for a brief moment. Dad reached for her ... and lost his fight with the water. The car lurched like a metal crocodile, driving him down in the water. His hand appeared by Mom's, then they both disappeared as the Taurus floated over them, tilted, and sank as water poured into the open windows. I saw it flip in the raging brown water, its bumper flashing silver like a leaping fish, then it disappeared.

The water continued to rise until it lapped at my still feet. The dry wash had become a raging river. Debris flashed downstream. To me, it looked like lost dreams and hopes carried away by the power of the world.

Through all of this I was held motionless, unable to move, or feel, until both Mom and Dad disappeared. I felt Mom's last thought of wanting to see me, and Dad's despair of losing both the drugs and Mom. They were small flashes of pain, and regret — of wishes that now would never come true.

For a moment, there was a last wish, a final spark, and then they were gone. A last touch, a fading grasp at life. I was stunned by it all. All the pain, all the fear, the disbelief, the sense of loss, and the reluctant acceptance.

They were gone. Fifteen years of not knowing, fifteen years of "what if?", all of it, gone in one night. I don't know how long I sat there, watching the muddy brown flood rise, roil, then fall away as the water disappeared into the thirsty ground like a fading memory. The dry wash was once again a pristine sand bed: no plants, animals, car, or people.

Coyotes howled in the distance. The noise was unnerving. The cacophony of their voices matching the turmoil inside me as I tried to make sense of the nightmare. Noise.

I opened my eyes. The sun was still below the horizon. The sky was a clear yellow blue to the east, a dark blue violet to the west. Overhead was the deep, pastel blue of the coming dawn. I was sitting in the middle of the dry wash, near a half-buried portion of a large branch, or small tree.

A few small birds darted by, starting their own day of finding food. The only noise was the wind blowing softly, and a last fading howl of a coyote. I pushed myself upright, and faced the direction I dreamed Mom and Dad floated away with the Taurus. The piece of ground I was standing on was the place in my dream where I saw the Taurus disappear under the raging water. I shivered as a chill ran up my spine.

Was this the place? Were they buried here under the sand?

The sense of conviction that this was true had to stem from the dream, but I couldn't shake the feeling that they were there, under the sand. There was one way to find out: my metal detector. If the Taurus was here, there should be a large signal from the detector.

I slowed as I got back to my camp. Silence enveloped me. The wind had died, and I heard none of the typical morning sounds. It seemed that the whole area was holding its breath. All of its attention was on me, and waiting for what I was to do. The sense of a strange, life-altering moment felt heavy upon me — a diverging path that would define my direction in life.

I saw things in two distinct possibilities. One, I would find the Taurus, know my dream was a true past seeing, and move forward in a life that always hunted answers and reasons why. Or, I could let go of it all. Say goodbye to their mystery, and call my vivid experience just a dream, and move forward in the life I'd begun for myself.

Follow them, and hunt more answers, or let go and follow an unknown path. My hand was on the metal detector. It would be a simple thing to confirm that the dream was a true seeing. All I would have to do was use the detector. I could use it, and let go, say goodbye, knowing they weren't lost ... or so I told myself. It would be so simple; and it was so tempting. I could prove my dream. Prove to myself that my Mom and Dad were ...

I looked at the metal detector in my hand once again. A sudden soft breeze floated past me. Warmer than the air around me, it enveloped me like an embrace of a lover — or a parent. My eyes blurred with tears and my heart clenched.

My hand, still gripping the metal detector tightly, trembled. I closed my eyes, blinking the tears away, and made my decision.

ABOUT THE AUTHOR

J Dark is a latecomer to the writing profession, but enjoying every moment that life will allow. "The best thing to me is writing a story that someone enjoys. If I've made something fun and entertaining for people, it's a win-win."

The author lives with a house full of dreams, three cats, and various friends who occasionally drop by and stay for a while. The author lives in Kansas, where the winds blow all the time, and, if you blink your eyes, the weather changes.

J Dark is the author of the "Glass Bottles" series and the short story collection, *Sometimes After Dark.* You can find out more about their work at *The Pandemonium* (*thepandemonium.net*).

YOU MIGHT ALSO ENJOY

BEST SERVED COLD

by Bob Schoonover

A dish of corporate greed served with a side of revenge.

PARRISH BLUE

by Vanessa MacLaren-Wray

Sallie never expected to discover a world she'd forgotten how to imagine.

REDUCTION IN FORCE

by Steve Soult

A heartless corporate layoff leaves Gil Schaffer emotionally shattered.

Available in digital and trade paperback editions from
Water Dragon Publishing
waterdragonpublishing.com

www.ingramcontent.com/pod-product-compliance
Lightning Source LLC
Chambersburg PA
CBHW051303190726
48286CB00004B/1238